Jacqueline Derbyshire was born in Wallasey, Merseyside. She left home at a young age working predominantly in health and social care, now back to her roots. Always wanting to write books but never having the time, that opportunity presented itself in 2020 when the world changed for all.

Living in a time of uncertainty, imagination can only bring joy. Sharing this journey of love, healing and magic, the author offers you insight into a wondrous world within a world.

THE ROADSIDE FAIRIES

Elder

JACQUELINE DERBYSHIRE

AUSTIN MACAULEY PUBLISHERS™

LONDON • CAMBRIDGE • NEW YORK • SHARJAH

Copyright © Jacqueline Derbyshire (2021)

A CIP catalogue record for this title is available from the British Library.

ISBN 9781398423824 (Paperback)
ISBN 9781398423831 (ePub e-book)

www.austinmacauley.com

First Published (2021)
Austin Macauley Publishers Ltd
25 Canada Square
Canary Wharf
London
E14 5LQ

I would like to dedicate this book to my mum, Norma Derbyshire. Never forgotten and missed every single day, her love and caring ways inspire me to be the best I can be.

Thank you to my husband, Rodney Finnigan, and my nephew, Daniel Foley, who live with me and have had to listen to me being so enthusiastic about writing this book, even when they didn't want to listen.

Prologue

Back in the day when there were no cars or other vehicles, only horsepower, there were just pathways created by nature. There lived groups or dwellings of the roadside fairies, living in different locations across the land.

The fairy realms all gathered once a year to celebrate their good fortunes and to share old and new spells to be considered by the Elders.

The fairies followed the guidance of three books: *The Book of Understanding; The Book of Teaching and Knowledge and the third and most sacred book, The Book of the Elders.*

The Elders were only allowed to read the books or to teach from them. However, the only book they would not teach from was *The Book of the Elders*, since this book contained dark magic and was only used by the Elders when required.

Young fairies were taught very early to cast spells of healing as this was deemed their primary role. These spells were shared from *The Book of Understanding* and *The Book of Teaching and Knowledge*. Over the years, new spells and incantations were sought and, if proven to be useful, would be added into *The Book of Teaching and Knowledge* to be shared.

The three books were held by the most trusted of the Elders called the 'Great Elder'. Their role was to ensure the safety and security of the books so as not to be misused for personal use and for any fairies to gain access into dark magic. All of the Great Elders had a trusted animal called a 'Guardian' whom they could confide in and trust.

The fairies of the realms predominant role were to heal the creatures of the land when they were ill or sustained injuries. Potions would be used and spells would be performed to heal. The creatures understood that the fairies were there help them and over many years had become able to communicate with them.

THE ROADSIDE FAIRIES   6

In return for their help, the creatures would provide plants and herbs they required for the potions required. All was as it should be perfectly balanced and Mother Nature providing for all.

Unfortunately, over time, things changed dramatically for the fairies and the creatures as people started to invent and build vehicles that required roads large and small. Major roadways appeared in time with vehicles that were very fast and dangerous with acrid fumes filling the air.

The fairies and the creatures were constantly having to readjust to this danger and move their dwellings and homes to stay as safe as they could be. Cautiously they did this and over time the fairy dwellings dwindled to twelve across the lands.

The fairies' role was now more important than ever to help the creatures, as more and more were being hurt or killed on the roads and at the roadsides.

With this, some of the younger fairies were becoming more and more resistant to the old ways, endeavouring along a passage of unrest and wanting to use dark spells and magic.

The three books were under constant threat of being taken and especially *The Book of the Elders*, where the rouge fairies knew there was dark magic to be acquired. Fairies once friendly and harmonious were turning sly, secretive and devious.

Characters

Greenwood
Beatri	Great Elder male
Tapi	Elder female
Birdia	Elder male

Young fairies
Eru	(Earth) female
Woosh	(Wind) male
Fute	(Fire) female
Wim	(Water) male
Aruf	(Air) female

Limes
Yendor	male
Treb	male
Knock	male
Willow	female
Putii older Lime fairy	female

Evestree
Namote	Great Elder male
Laroc	Elder female
Sidar	Elder female

Limes
Ytrunse	male
Jist	female
Sanwin	male
Beru	male

Creatures Greenwood
Chati   crow (Guardian)
Suni   squirrel
Shade   squirrel
Cervi   deer

Mustelid badger
Queen Bee Melissa

Creatures Evestree
Gloss   crow (Guardian)

Creatures in cahoots with Limes dark magic
Petra magpie leader

Hep wood pigeon leader
Slu toad leader

Attenberry family
Live in commune in forest close to Greenwood dwelling Clover
Dad Cervide   (Cerv)
Mum Serendipity   (Serp)
Grandfather Stargazer   (Star)
Grandmother Namioi   (Nam)

Brother Fig
Bertie Pug dog   (Clovers)

Humans called (crags) by fairies and creatures

Chapter 1
The Book of the Elders

Beatri, the Great Elder of Greenwood, was troubled by the undercurrents of mischief and deviousness starting to occur and could sense the unrest of some of the older fairies known as Limes. Information was being communicated to him by creatures deep in the forest hearing secret meetings taking place. Unfortunately spells had been cast so that the creatures could not distinguish who was in attendance.

Beatri decided that *The Book of the Elders* was in threat of being taken for use other than its purpose, so he decided action must be taken to ensure its safety and called on his Guardian creature, Chati the crow, whom he trusted above all others.

Beatri went into the forest alone and unseen and by casting incantations of old he used his magic and cast many spells on *The Book of the Elders*, and it turned into a tree that looked old and inhabited. Beatri informed Chati where the tree was and that he must protect it at any cost and to keep its location secret. Chati immediately took action and called upon his friends Suni and Shade, the squirrels whom he knew he could trust. Suni and Shade were asked to stay at the tree and not to leave at any cost until Chati would return to get updated reports and allow them to rest.

Chapter 2
Roadside Fairies

Due to the ever-increasing incidents happening by the roadsides, the fairies had become very busy concocting potions and setting up healing lodgings where their treatments of spells would be administered to creatures injured by the roadsides.

Daily teachings took place where the fairies learnt to cast spells and make potions. There were different levels of knowledge provided, depending on the age and skills of the fairies. There were also the important teachings of rejuvenation techniques taught, as when they casted spells depending on the power required, the fairies became tired and their magic and abilities depleted.

Younger fairies who wore silver gowns were at an early stage of understanding and would only assist the older fairies.

The older fairies called Limes wore lime-green robes and had larger wings and were stronger. They knew more in-depth spells and incantations and led on the nightly journeys to the roadsides.

Every evening there would be a full meeting at Greenwood where the Elders would meet to discuss the issues of the day and other information passed on from the creatures living in the forest. Teams were delegated their roles of where to go to attend to the creatures reported injured, reporting to the injured creature's family and ensuring they were supported. The fairies predominantly worked at night when the roads were quieter, and they had less chance of being seen by the crags. The fairies all had the ability to light the end of their wings so they could see by using an incantation. Also, the creatures could see them and were always happy to do so as they knew what they were doing, healing their fellow creatures.

Beatri, Tapi and Birdia would discuss the security of the nectar supplies as this was the fairy's elixir. This task was tendered to by a small group of fairies who worked around the clock to keep the stocks up. The fairies also supported the bees and shared a certain amount with them. Queen Bee Melissa took charge of the logistics and would produce a special honey that was gifted to the fairies yearly for the annual gathering.

Chapter 3
The Five Young Fairies

The youngest fairies living at Greenwood were called Eru, Woosh, Fute, Wim and Aruf. They were friends and would spend their free time together. Their names meant:

Eru – earth
Woosh – wind
Fute – fire
Wim – water
Aruf – air

Their names were given to the fairies depending on the time they were rejuvenated. These names were taken from *The Book of the Elders*. The names have been passed down over the centuries. Eru was the cleverest fairy, she listened intently to all of the teachings. Woosh was a strong fairy and showed great prowess as a future Elder. Fute was a sensitive fairy who would follow her friends wherever they went or whatever they did; however, she was able to use the strongest magic in secret. Wim was the joker, looking to have fun and always cheering his friends up. Aruf was the docile fairy, she always got confused and ended up in trouble. Unfortunately, her magic skills were somewhat questionable (Always going wrong). Her strength was her foresight and she had a gift of seeing into the future. Aruf did not share this gift with her friends as she didn't understand them herself. Aruf was always found sneaking nectar from the storage. This made her rather bigger and heavier than her friends.

Chapter 4
The Limes

Part of the older group of fairies who had recently passed their magic and spell teachings would now be selected to have access into *The Book of Teaching and Knowledge* and *The Book of Understanding*. They would not, however, have access to The Book of the Elders. This was book was specifically for the chosen, as it contained dark magic and spells from old times that the fairies did not practice. These fairies were called Limes and their names were: Treb, Willow, Xnock and Yendor.

Yendor was the leader of the group. The Greenwood Limes had a connection with other Limes from Evestree, and with the support of a wood pigeon named Hep and a magpie called Petra, the Limes would use the creatures by sending secret messages to each other back and forth. The Limes who lived in Evestree were called Ytruns, Sanwim, Jist and Beru. The main quest of the Limes was to gain access to *The Book of the Elders* so they could practice forbidden magic and spells.

Chapter 5
Clover

Clover was a ten-year-old young girl. She was very clever and inquisitive, constantly yearning to learn all she could. She lived with her family in the forest in a commune moving around with another group of people, living off the land. They were all vegetarians. Clover's father and grandfather were all very ingenious, brilliant at making things out of unused items such as fallen trees. They were able to build a home for the family wherever they ventured. Clover's mother and grandmother were extremely clever at concocting wondrous meals from foraging vegetables and growing herbs. The recipes had been handed down by the family over many years. There were many books in place written to guide them. They also prepared potions for healing; they saw this as their main role. Herbs and plants were collected and prepared for any situation. Clover and the younger children were taught by their parents and the Elders of the commune, teaching them all there was to learn about living alongside the creatures of the forest as they deemed it to be the creature's domain. The children were taught to protect themselves and to never leave the commune by themselves. If they did, they must be within sight and inform their parents of where they were venturing. Clover loved venturing out collecting herbs and foliage for her potion-making. Her father had made her a basket to carry them in.

Clover really looked forward to the evening when all the commune grouped together and stories would be told about their ancestors all of whom had lived in forests across the world. Stories such as the roadside fairies who had tiny lights on their wings so they were able to see in the dark. The Roadside fairies' main objective was to help injured creatures. The fairies performed great spells of healing and in turn they lived harmonious lives with the creatures, learning to communicate with each other over the years. The people from the communes had seen the fairies but only a snapshot. As soon as people spotted them, the fairy lights went out and they disappeared.

Chapter 6
Clover Goes into the Forest

Clover completed her daily teachings and was helping her mum and grandmother along with others to check the stocks for their potions. Serp had written a list of herbs that they were required to stock up on. Clover volunteered to go out foraging, taking her pug Bertie along with her. Serp allocated tasks to all of the youngsters, reiterating the rule of staying close to the commune. Clover gathered her basket and tools and walked off, with Bertie following close behind. They followed little pathways made by the creatures of the forest, careful not to disturb anything. Time passed quickly and Clover had found most of the herbs on her list and decided to take a little break. There in front of them was an old tree that looked like it was uninhabited as it wasn't as green and flourishing as the other trees. Clover sat down, leaning on the tree and checking her list whilst Bertie lay down and took a nap.

Clover could hear strange sounds that she was unfamiliar with, looking up to see two squirrels chattering away. Then all of a sudden, Clover could understand what they were saying. Suni and Shade were arguing about Suni going off to collect acorns as she had buried them not far from where they were. Shade was hungry but worried that if Suni left, Chati would find out and they would be in trouble. Clover was in awe and so excited about what she had heard and called up to Suni and Shade, saying, "Hello, how are you?"

The squirrels squealed when they saw Clover and even more so when they realised, they could understand this crag (human). Suni yelled, "Oh goodness, Chati will be so angry with us."

Shade spoke to Clover, asking, "Who are you?
Do you possess magic?"

Clover answered calmly but excitedly, "No. My name is Clover and I live over there with my family and friends." Suddenly Bertie ran over, barking. Clover exclaimed, "Oh my goodness, Bertie, I understand you too!"
Bertie replied, "Yes, yes, yes, isn't this amazing?"

The group were taken aback at this and all started to speak at the same time.

Clover then heard the chimes from the commune, commanding she return home. Clover stood up and told them she needed to leave.

Suni and Shade asked Clover not to share the destination of the tree or that a strange magic had taken place.
Clover crossed her arms over her chest and said, "Cross my heart and turn around – I swear your secret will not be found."
Bertie barked, "I won't tell either."

Clover left Suni and Shade, her mind in a whirl and so very excited, but she understood she had made a promise that she could not break. When just a few feet away from the tree, Bertie began barking and Clover could not understand him any longer. Suni and Shade agreed they would not tell Chati about the crag (for now anyway).

Chapter 7
The Recovery Lodge

Back at Greenwood, the younger fairies had completed their teachings and practices, and it was now their time to relax and enjoy their time together. Eru asked the group what they wanted to do, and they all agreed to go see the creatures who were recovering, wanting to talk to them as the group were very inquisitive and to ask them about the forest as they loved hearing about the creature's travels and how they had been injured by the roadside. Tapi and Birdia were in charge of the recovery lodgings ensuring that creatures could not be seen and that their recoveries were speedy, depending on the severity of their injuries. One of the injured creatures was Mustelid, a badger. He was crossing one of the roads the previous night and a crag's vehicle hit him on his side, hurting his back legs. Mustelid was very grateful to the roadside fairies as they acted quickly, casting their pain-relief spells and taking him to the recovery lodgings. Spells and potions were used and Mustelid was comfortable. Eru asked if the group could help by going to inform his family that he was doing well and would return home soon. Tapi informed Eru that this would be very beneficial as they hadn't been able to report it due to the very busy night before. The five fairies got excited at the task ahead, as they could wander into the forest unaccompanied. Aruf was a bit uneasy at this quest as she had had a vision the day before about Woosh and Win that had frightened her. The other fairies persuaded Aruf to join them, promising there would be some nectar to be sourced. Tapi informed them to stay safe, follow the rules, report back and not to wander off their task.

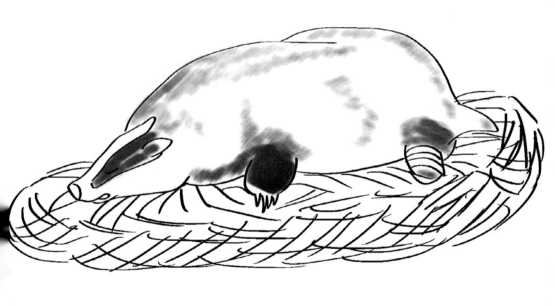

Chapter 8
The Limes Meet

Yendor had decided that they would meet to plan on how to gain possession of *The Book of the Elders*. Petra the magpie had bought communication from Evestree to inform the Limes there were ready to take action. The leader of the Limes at Evestree was Yturns: a bold Lime who had been showing signs of his discontent of the new ways. Since being a young fairy, the Great Elder leader Namote had observed Yturns turning and this worried him, especially as his group of Limes were able to produce strong spells. Yturns had also got Putii, one of the more older fairies involved in their tryst. Yturns had sent a message to Yendor, they were ready and they should meet at the next full moon the following evening. The location was given and Yendor requested that the Limes would use spells and magic so that the other fairies would not notice them missing.

Yendor had studied *The Book of Teaching and Knowledge* in secret and gained great insight, sharing this with the other Limes. He showed them spells but not all of them as he wanted to be the new Lime leader of the new dwelling.

Chapter 9
The Five Fairies Fly
Off into the Forest

Eru and the other fairies flew out into the forest following Mustelid's instructions to the location of his family. Excitedly they went ensuring they were not seen. Wim was constantly hiding and flying out to surprise the others. Enjoying this, Woosh decided he would hide too. Further along the two flew off. Eru was not amused and she ensured the other fairies stayed tight together and off they went. Aruf was getting tired and asked if they could rest for a little bit as she had seen some beautiful bushes full of flowers, thinking there was lovely nectar to be had. Aruf landed on the bush with Eru and Fute landing close by. Eru told Aruf that she must not eat too much nectar as they had little time left to complete their task.

Wim and Woosh had gone further into the forest, not realising the girls were not following them. Wim flew behind Woosh where they giggled and decided they would land on a tree and wait for the girls in hiding. Whilst waiting, they saw Petra the magpie with Hep the wood pigeon and they were deep in conversation. Wim was intrigued and said to Woosh, "Let's find out why they're meeting and what they're talking about."

Woosh was a bit unnerved but agreed, so quietly, they flew above the pair. What they heard was how Yendor and Ytruns were planning a meeting the following night when the moon was full and they wanted the creatures to meet with them as well as plans were being put into place to take over the forest. The other fairies had resumed their journey, Eru constantly worrying about where the two boys were, hoping they had carried on ahead to Mustelid's family. When the girls arrived, the two boys were nowhere to be seen. Eru informed the badgers of Mustelid's message and that he would return very soon healthy and well. The worried family exchanged genuine thanks with the fairies, and because of the lateness, the fairies had to say their goodbyes and return home to Greenwood. On the journey back, Wim and Woosh had decided to catch up with the girls and tell them of what they had overheard. Worried, frightened and in disbelief, they flew on.

Chapter 10
The Commune

Clover returned overly excited and her brother Fig picked up on it straight away, asking, "What's got into you, Clove? You look like you've hit the jackpot!"

Clover replied, "No, just happy as I have found all the herbs Mum needed."

Bertie was jumping up and down at Fig like an overexcited puppy.

Clover delivered the herbs to Serp and Nomioi, who were very pleased with her findings. Clover was told to prepare herself for the evening meal, which was ready. That evening, the commune gathered for the storytelling.

Clover wanted to shout out that she had been a part of some magic but kept her promise.

Chapter 11
Unrest in the Forest

Chati returned to the tree to check on Sunny and Shade and to allow them to take a break to go and get their acorns. Chati could sense there was an uneasiness, but nothing was reported so he got himself comfortable until they returned.

Beatri and Namote, both the Great Elders, sensed something was happening and decided to meet with the other Elders – Birdia, Tapi, Laroc and Sidar – to find out any information they had to share. Beatri was aware that spells had been used from *The Book of Teaching and Knowledge*'; however, the book was not disclosing who it was as a dark spell had been cast. Obviously with *The Book of the Elders*, the spell could be undone, but Beatri did not want to divulge its location.

In the forest, Cervi, the great deer, had heard of creatures becoming sly and mischievous and he himself, whilst drinking from the stream, had heard the frogs talking mischievously about a new leader amongst the fairies. Slu, the frog leader, was boasting about the frogs being part of the takeover and was excited to follow the new fairy Lime leader. Hep and Petra had informed Slu that the new Lime leader knew strong magic and had promised to share it with them all.

Cervi was unnerved listening to the conversation and ran off into the forest, heading to the dwelling of Beatri at Greenwood. That evening the Elders discussed the oncoming challenge, they knew Yendor and Ytruns were up to no good and they knew that other Limes had joined them. They discussed a plan, keeping it amongst themselves to stop the revolt. Beatri was the only one who knew where *The Book of the Elders* was and told the other Elders he would not disclose the whereabouts to protect the dwellings.

Chapter 12
Greenwood

The Elders organised the fairies for their evening roles of going to the roadsides to check for injured creatures. This included the Limes, as their role was to ensure the younger fairies' safety. The Limes also had the spells and magic of healing and transport spells for the creatures injured ensuring, they got them to the recovery lodgings.

Cervi arrived at Greenwood and requested an audience with Beatri as he had very important information to share. Beatri met with Cervi in private and listened to the conversation he had overheard, and Cervi informed him of the whispers in the forest of unrest and of a new leader living in one the fairy dwellings.
Beatri thanked Cervi, his old friend, and asked him not to divulge the information to anyone, and asked him to listen out in the forest for any other communication by the creatures turning towards evil. Cervi left the dwelling concerned for their safety as he knew too well of the consequences when bad magic and evil spells were performed.

Chapter 13
The Great Elders' Plan

Later that evening, Beatri and Namote met with all of the other Elders at the secret location only known to them. Namote began by informing them that he believed that the Limes were in cahoots and named the Limes he knew to be led by Ytruns at Evestree. Beatri informed them of the Limes led by Yendor and also Putii at Greenwood. The Elders were very worried as they knew dark magic and spells would be used by the Limes as they had taken them from *The Book of Teaching and Knowledge* and *The Book of Understanding* and had been able to strengthen their capabilities. Concerned for the other fairies and creatures as they would inevitably be hurt, a plan was put together and the Elders left, returning to their dwellings to initiate it immediately.

Chapter 14
The Takeover Plot

Yendor met with the other Limes as planned the following evening just before the moon was at its brightest. This was when the fairies felt the moon's force and its imminent power that rejuvenated them. Yendor showed them some dark magic spells by debilitating some creatures close by, and they were now unable to move. The other Limes shouted with glee and clapped, encouraging Yendor to show them more. Yturns in turn showed off his abilities by casting spells of fire, reducing foliage to ashes with speed. The Limes cheered and awaited their instructions. The decision was to take over one dwelling at a time and to start at Greenwood. Yendor and Yturns taught the others spells that would weaken the younger fairies. They themselves would tackle the Elders. The plan was to imprison them and decide what to do with them once the dwelling was theirs.

Yendor and Yturns discussed the taking of *The Book of the Elders* and knew their quest was going to be difficult as the Great Elders would not part with it easily. They also discussed Putii, an older fairy Lime, who had sided with them. Putii had tried to further herself into leadership as an Elder but was rebuked by the Great Elders as they said she was still not worthy for the role. This had infuriated Putii and when she became aware of Yendor's plan to take over, she immediately joined the Limes.

Putii had the role of watching and following Beatri in secret, this she did and patiently and secretly for what seemed like a very long time. Putii believed she knew the whereabouts of *The Book of the Elders* and had informed Beatri.

Chapter 15
The Tree

Clover lay awake as the moon was very bright and decided it wouldn't be difficult to just go and see Suni and Shade for a few minutes. Off she went quietly, with Bertie running behind her excited that they were able to see the path they needed to take. Clover had taken some of her potions to show the squirrels what she could do with them.

When Clover arrived, Suni and Shade were resting in the tree. When Clover shouted out to them, they became startled but were happy to see the little crag and her dog.

Eru and the other friends met to discuss what they should do. Aruf then told them of her dream that Greenwood was under imminent danger and fairies were going to be hurt. Aruf was very specific and the group believed her. Fute then told them of her ability to cast special magic that would render them invisible for short periods of time. The group were in awe when Fute showed them. Feeling that they were need back at their dwelling, they flew off and decided to go to tell Beatri.

The fairies found Beatri and quickly informed him of what Woosh and Wim had overheard and of Aruf's visions. Beatri had been watching the group of fairies and overtime he was aware of their strengths and abilities. As a Great Elder, Beatri had insight to the fairies' capabilities and part of his role was to receive information from the teachers and mentors who would be trusted fairies and he believed these five fairies to be special.

Beatri set them a task to go to the tree in the forest where they would be required to protect the tree and the creatures who were acting as its caretaker. Beatri did not inform the group why the tree was so important but trusted them to follow his orders. Beatri also sent his trusted crow Chati to keep Suni and Shade safe.

Chapter 16
The Limes Attack
Greenwood

Greenwood fairies had started to settle in for the rest of the night, having enjoyed the evening, when they heard and saw the Limes appear suddenly, casting lightning-fast spells.

The spells caused the younger fairies to fall to the ground, unable to move. Beatri and the Elders' counterattack and there was a lot of strong magic used. Yendor had seen the group of fairies flying off unaware of their task and sent a couple of lower-level Limes to follow and capture them. The group arrived at the tree the same time as Chati and then were attacked by the Limes who had followed them. Spells were cast; however, Fute casted her magic and the five fairies disappeared. The Limes started casting spells at the creatures in the tree. Clover and Bertie couldn't believe their eyes and ran to the tree. Clover tripped over and one of her potions spilled out. The potion possessed strong magic and a veil of light smoke covered the tree. The Limes became unable to use any spells against them. The five fairies then flew behind the Limes unseen and casted spells. With Eru's and Fute's abilities, they were able to wrap the Limes in an invisible binding, wrapping it around them and they fell to the ground.

Chapter 17
Chaos at Greenwood

The Limes were struggling against the strength of the Elders, and with Yendor's orders, they used the fire spells aiming at the beehives that were all around the dwelling. This caused pandemonium. The bees, disorientated, left their hives and led by their queen Melissa flew off into the forest away from the fires.

Putii informed Yendor of the whereabouts of *The Book of the Elders*. Beatri left Yturns with the other Limes and they flew off in the direction Putii believed it to be. Unbeknownst to her, Beatri had set up a trap knowing her to have followed him for some reason and it was now clear it was for the book.

They flew into an old cave close by that was hidden from sight knowing strong magic had been used excitedly they flew deeper in. Hiding unseen were two Elders from Evestree, Laroc and Sidar, who bombarded the pair with extraordinary powerful magic, spells that had not been used since days of old. They captured Yendor and Putii, who were totally unprepared for such power to be used against them.

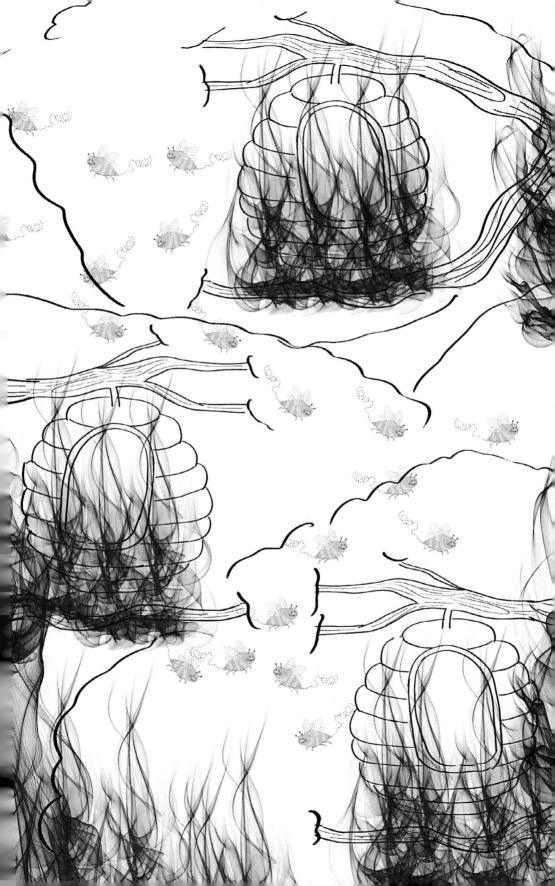

Chapter 18
Gathering at the Tree

Clover's mother checked in on her to find her bed empty and Bertie also missing. She informed Cervide, her husband, and Clover's grandparents. They left the commune. Cerv and Star took the lead as they were very apt at following tracks. They followed the path Clover and Bertie had taken. In no time they reached the forest and could see the tree with Clover and Bertie underneath it and to their amazement could see what was taking place with fairies flying around. Clover was standing by the tree with Bertie and was talking to Chati and the squirrels who were thanking her for her great magic. Just then one of the Limes was able to cast a spell, setting the tree on fire. Cerv and Star rushed over and put the fire out quickly, scorching their hands in the process. Serp and Grandmother Namioi took out potions from their coats that healed their hands and they also applied some onto the burnt part of the tree.

Clover ran into her mother's arms trying to explain why she had left the commune when all of a sudden the area was filled with thousands of bees following Queen Bee Melissa. Chati flew out to Melissa who told him of their hives being burnt down and having to find a safe place for the swarm. Chati informed Clover and the others of their dilemma and later Clover told her family of what had been taking place. Cerv and Star advised her to tell Chati to inform the bees that they would build them new hives.

Beatri flew to the tree and saw the amazing sight of the crags standing by the tree and the Limes who had been captured by the young fairies. Chati flew to Beatri and informed him of Clover's magic and how she had protected them and the tree. Clover understood Beatri, who thanked her for her braveness and actions. Beatri informed the five fairies to return to Greenwood with the captured Limes and he would return imminently. Chati informed Beatri of the crags volunteering to make hives for the bees and asked Clover to thank them. The group were then asked to meet at the tree the following night.

Beatri asked Chati and the squirrels to remain at the tree for one more night, to which they agreed.

Beatri returned to Greenwood where Cervi and other creatures were helping the young fairies and the Elders were casting spells to eradicate the magic performed on them by the Limes. Beatri and Yturns organised the Limes and other revolters be locked in lodgings where they would be seen to. Then the fairies were designated roles to build up Greenwood to its former safe haven.

The five fairies were thanked by the Great Elders for their contribution in saving the tree and also of their strength and honour reporting to Beatri at a crucial time. The fairies were very excited and honoured to have gained the trust of the Elders, a great thing indeed! Aruf asked whether there was a reward in the way of some nectar; the other fairies all hugged Aruf and they all giggled.

Chapter 19
Evening Meeting
Back at the Tree

Cerv and Star worked through the night and next day with the support of the men at the commune, not telling them the real reason, as they understood the importance of keeping the roadside fairies a secret.

Clover and Bertie slept late into the morning as they were exhausted by their antics the night before, then waking up excitedly looking forward to seeing her newfound friends that evening.

That evening the hives were loaded into a cart and, as not to disturb too much of the pathway, was pulled by Cerv and Star, not too difficult a task, and they kept the cutting of shrubbery to a minimal.

Clover, Bertie, Serp and Nom walked behind, all excited to see the fairies. They also had potions to share with them, including the one that protected the tree. Clover was to read out the ingredients to Chati who would inform Beatri.

Arriving at the tree, Clover and Bertie ran over, waving and informing Chati and the squirrels of their arrival. They were all happy to see each other. Conversations immediately took place with the five, even Bertie was running in whirlies and barking out his hellos.

Beatri arrived with the other elders from Greenwood and the five fairy friends as Beatri thought it only right to invite them as they were the ones who had also played a part in protecting the tree and Chati and the squirrels.

Beatri saw the hives and told Chati to thank the Attenberrys and that they would deliver them to Queen Bee Melissa. Clover was still standing close by the tree with Bertie, while the others were standing a bit further away. Beatri and the Elders started flying around the family casting spells and incantations. Within seconds, the Attenberrys turned around and walked back following the path used to the commune.

Clover and Bertie, however, did not leave with them.

Beatri asked Chati and the squirrels to leave the tree and requested that Clover and Bertie move away. Beatri flew around the tree for what seemed ages when all of a sudden, the tree was covered in a white plume no longer visible to all observing. The plume dissipated and Beatri flew out, carrying *The Book of the Elders*, and the tree had disappeared. All watching were in awe and then the fairies and creatures observing understood why the tree had to be protected at all costs.

To Clover and astonishment, she could still understand Chati, Clover was thanked and informed by Chati that their paths would cross again. Bertie had fallen asleep, it had been far too much excitement for him. Clover woke Bertie and they returned home very tired indeed!

Chapter 20
All Is Well at Greenwood

The hives were delivered to the bees who were so very grateful, and Queen Bee Melissa thanked them, taking the lead to move into the hives immediately.

All had settled down in Greenwood restored to its former safe, comfortable dwelling.

All was as it should have been, and the Elders were organising the fairies for their nightly roles as creatures had to be rescued and healed from the roadsides. The Elders had all agreed that *The Book of the Elders* should once again be hidden, and this task was given to Namote, the Great Elder at Evestree.

The five fairies all had been honoured by the Elders and had been sent to a higher level of learning where they would learn a higher level of spells and magic, and more responsibility in healing and helping injured creatures at the roadsides.

Chapter 21
The Secret Is Safe

Clover returned to the commune, Bertie by her side, and was asked by her mum Serp if she had enjoyed her walk. It seemed that all of the Attenberrys had no memory of what had just occurred. Clover looked at Bertie, winked and said, "Amazing, thank you."

Clover wrote herself a little rhyme to remember her creature and fairy friends:

The roadside fairies' the roadside fairies they come out at night.
The roadside fairies twinkle in the moon light.

The roadside fairies, oh, what a sight, healing the creatures at the roadside with the creatures' great delight.

The roadside fairies, the roadside fairies, spot them if you can, little stars by the roadside, be quick because if you look twice, they have gone.

Descriptions of Characters

Characters

Greenwood

Beatri   Great Elder male

White beard and long hair, small blue eyes, large nose, big ears
Long dark green gown with a hood to cover to feet, big pockets
at front, bare large feet. Very large wings.

Tapi   Elder female

Grey hair in bun, blue round eyes, soft features, a lighter shade
of green robe. Large wings but not as big as Beatri.

Birdia   Elder male

Grey hair long, short beard, small blue eyes, big straight nose, a
lighter shade of green robe. Large wings but not as big as Beatri.

Young fairies

Euru (Earth)   Female

Dark brown hair long, big blue eyes, small build, small nose,
pretty, silver gown to the knees, small wings.

Whoosh (Wind)   Male

Dark brown hair short, small blue eyes, pointy nose, silver robe
to feet, small wings.

Fute (Fire)   Female

Blonde hair long, big blue eyes, small build, small nose, pretty,
silver gown to the knees, small wings.

Wim (Water)   Male
Dark brown hair short, big blue eyes, small nose, big ears, silver robe to feet, small wings.

Aruf (Air)   Female
Dark brown hair long and bushy, big blue eyes, rotund build, small nose, very pretty, silver gown to the knees, small wings.

Limes
Yendor   Male
Larger than young fairies, lime green robe to feet, blonde hair in ponytail, dark eyes, pointy nose, fierce looking, larger wings that fairies.

Treb   Male
Larger than young fairies, lime green robe to feet, dark hair short, blue eyes, pointy nose, none descript, larger wings that fairies.

Knock   Male
Larger than young fairies, lime green robe to feet, dark hair short, blue eyes, pointy nose, none descript, larger wings that fairies.

Willow   Female
Larger than young fairies, lime green robe to knees, dark hair long, blue eyes, pointy nose, none descript, larger wings that fairies.

Putii   Female

Older Lime Fairy, larger than young fairies, lime green robe to feet, long white hair, blue eyes, large pointy nose, slightly larger wings that fairies and Limes but not as big as elders.

Evestree
Namote   Great Elder Male
White beard and long hair in ponytail, small blue eyes, large nose, small ears and a disguised mole on chin. Long dark green gown with a hood, big pockets at front. Very large wings.

Laroc   Elder Female
Grey hair in plait, blue round eyes, soft features, a lighter shade of green robe. Large wings but not as big as Beatri.

Sidar   Elder Female
Grey hair long, small blue eyes, big straight nose, a lighter shade of green robe. Large wings but not as big as Beatri.

Limes with same descriptions as Yendor and others with a few differences to each one
Ytrunse   Male
Jist   Female
Sanwin   Male
Beru   Male

Greenwood Creatures
Chati   crow (Guardian) Big black shiny crow

Suni   squirrel, female, red and big bushy tail
Shade   squirrel, male Red with smaller tail

Cervi   deer, big, powerful and magnificent

Mustelid   badger big and strong with soft features
Queen Bee Melissa magnificent

Creatures in cahoots with Limes dark magic
Petra   magpie, leader. nasty looking
Hep   wood pigeon, leader, fat bird
Slu   frog leader, fat, with big mouth

Attenberry family
Live in commune in forest close to Greenwood dwelling Clover
Red hair very long in plaits with big green eyes, round face, pale
skin, small frame.
Wearing denim shorts, blue T-shirt and pumps.

Dad Cervide (Cerv)
Tall dark haired in pony, green eyes, middle aged.
Wearing denim overalls and boots

Mum Serendipity (Serp)
Red, short hair going grey, smiling green eyes, slim and petite.
Wearing jeans and T-shirt and pumps.

Grandfather Stargazer (Star)
Tall, grey haired, short beard, green eyes, wears glasses, older aged.
Wearing denim overalls and boots.

Grandmother Namioi (Nam)
Grey hair in bun, smiling green eyes, happy plump face,
quite rotund.
Wearing flowery dress with an apron over the top, with lots of
pockets and bottles in them. Sandals on feet.

Brother Fig
Tall blonde haired short, blue eyes, young good-looking teenager with acne.
Wearing denim jeans and T-shirt with training shoes.

Bertie   Pug dog, beige and black markings